Zac's Wild Rescue
published in 2009 by
Hardie Grant Egmont
85 High Street
Prahran, Victoria 3181, Australia
www.hardiegrantegmont.com.au

*The pages of this book are printed on paper derived
from forests promoting sustainable management.*

A CiP record for this title is available from the National Library of Australia

Text, illustration and design copyright © 2009 Hardie Grant Egmont

Printed in Australia by McPherson's Printing Group

9 10 8

ZAC'S WILD RESCUE

BY H. I. LARRY

**ILLUSTRATIONS BY ANDY HOOK,
RON MONNIER & ASH OSWALD**

hardie grant EGMONT

CHAPTER...
...ONE

Zac was in the school library. He had a science project to work on but he was bored. Zac didn't like doing projects.

He always left them to the last minute.

Zac was 12 years old. But he was not an ordinary kid. He was a spy for a group called GIB. Zac's code name was Agent Rock Star.

Spying was top secret.

The only people who knew Zac was a spy were his family, because they were spies too! Even Zac's dog, Agent Woofy, was a spy.

AGENT / WOOFY /
BREED / CLASSIFIED
FAVOURITE SNACK / BONE
AGE IN DOG YEARS / 54 / HUMAN YEARS / 7

Zac went on all sorts
of cool missions.
He was GIB's test
driver. This meant he
got to test drive all
the cool gadgets. He
got to go to awesome
places like outer space
and underwater. And
sometimes he had to

stop the evil spy group
called BIG from doing
bad things.

Zac wished his science
project was a top-secret
spy mission instead.
He looked around the
library and went over
to the shelves.
One book looked good.

It was called, *A Secret Agent's Spy Book*.

Zac took a closer look. The book had GIB written on it.

'Maybe it's a secret message,' Zac said.

said the librarian.

She didn't like noise
in the library.

Zac tried to pull the
book from the shelf.
It was stuck. Zac pulled
as hard as he could.
He heard a sound.
Something clicked
like a switch.

Suddenly the bookshelf began to move!

It was turning around. And Zac was going with it! The floor was moving with the bookshelf.

Cool, thought Zac.

Then the floor stopped moving. Zac wasn't in the library anymore.

Now he was in a
dark room.

'Hello?' Zac called out.
'Is anyone here?'

Then Zac heard his
brother's voice.
'Hello, Zac.'

'Hi, Leon,' said Zac.
'Where am I?'

CHAPTER... ...TWO

'This is a GIB Test Lab,' said Leon. He switched on the light so Zac could see.

'This secret room is awesome,' said Zac.

Leon was a spy, too. His code name was Agent Tech Head. Leon was in charge of the GIB Test Labs.

'GIB needs you to do some test driving,' said Leon.

'Cool,' said Zac. 'I am sick of my science project.'

Leon was holding something. It looked like a little bomb. It was the size of a shirt button.

'This is a Pit Stink Bomb,' said Leon.

'GIB wants them tested today.'

'What do you do with them?' asked Zac.

'You stick them under your armpits. To set them off you do the chicken dance with your arms. The bomb will crack open.

And it will
let out a
really bad smell!
The worst smell ever!'
Leon laughed.

'Gross!' said Zac.
'But they're very cool.'

'I've made a new suit, too,' said Leon. 'I call it the Exo-skeleton suit. What do you think?'

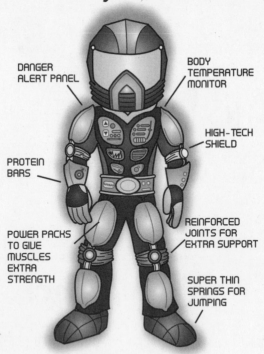

DANGER ALERT PANEL

BODY TEMPERATURE MONITOR

HIGH-TECH SHIELD

PROTEIN BARS

POWER PACKS TO GIVE MUSCLES EXTRA STRENGTH

REINFORCED JOINTS FOR EXTRA SUPPORT

SUPER THIN SPRINGS FOR JUMPING

Zac looked at the suit. It was big and heavy. It had a helmet.

'It doesn't look very comfy,' said Zac. 'Will I be able to move in it OK?'

'This suit will make you super strong,' said Leon.

'You'll be able to run very fast, too. And it has a shield that will protect you. Try it on.' Leon handed Zac the suit.

Zac put the Exo-skeleton suit on. It was easy to climb into. And it felt really light. Zac was surprised.

'It feels like I'm in my pyjamas!' Zac grinned. 'It's great.'

Zac put the helmet on. Then he felt a . . .

A tingle raced up Zac's back. 'What was that?' he asked.

'It's the suit fitting onto your body,' said Leon. 'Now it's ready to work.'

Something beeped inside Zac's pocket.

BEEP-BEEP-BEEP
BEEP-BEEP-BEEP

It was his GIB SpyPad. It was a mission from GIB.

TOP SECRET
FOR THE EYES OF ZAC POWER ONLY

MISSION SENT THURSDAY 3PM

The evil spy group BIG
is at the zoo.
They are setting the
animals free!
You must get to the zoo
and stop the animals
from escaping.
END

CHAPTER...
...THREE

'You can test drive the
Pit Stink Bombs on
the mission,' said Leon.
'And don't forget to do
your test drive report.'

Zac groaned as he took the Pit Stink Bombs. He loved missions, but he didn't like writing reports. They were almost as bad as school projects!

'Come over to the get-away tube,' said Leon.

'What's that?' asked Zac.

'Look, see the tunnel?' said Leon. 'It goes all the way back up to the ground above us. Step in.'

Zac stepped inside the tunnel. He could see the sky. But it was a long way up.

'How do I get up
there?' Zac called out.

'Jump,' called Leon.
'That suit will help
you jump super high!'

Zac did a huge jump

and flew up the tube.
He shot out the top
like a rocket!

Zac landed on the
school oval. He looked
for the get-away tube.
It was gone.

GIB has hidden it, Zac
thought. *Spy work has
to be top secret.*

Zac ran across the oval.

BOOM BOOM BOOM!

He was moving very fast. *Leon was right,* Zac thought. *I am super fast in this suit.*

Zac jumped over the school fence and ran for the zoo. The suit gave him super strength.

It made him run very fast. Zac jumped over cars and trucks.

He reached the zoo in no time. Zac jumped over the zoo gates.

There were people everywhere.

The people were screaming and running

all over the place.
The animals were
out of their cages.
It was CRAZY
inside the zoo!

CHAPTER... ...FOUR

Suddenly, Leon's face popped up on Zac's SpyPad. 'You need to get the people out of the zoo, Zac!' said Leon.

'They aren't safe.
Not with the animals
on the loose.'

'I know, but how?'
said Zac.

Then he remembered
the Pit Stink Bombs. He
pushed his arms down
against his body and did
the chicken dance.

He heard the bombs crack open.

Zac lifted his arms up. Gas flew out from his armpits.

WHOOSH!

The smell was really bad. It was the worst thing Zac had ever smelt.

Even worse then Agent Tool Belt's smells! Zac thought. Agent Tool Belt was Zac's dad.

The gas spread through the zoo. All the people held their noses.
The whole zoo stank! All the animals ran back to their cages.
The people began to run through the zoo gates. Zac closed the gates behind them.

*That was easy. But it
sure stinks in here!*
Zac thought as he
held his nose.

Zac walked around.
That's weird, thought
Zac. *Everything looks OK.*
But he could hear
something strange.

He kept walking.

And then Zac saw it.
A huge rhino! It was
on the path.

And it was headed
straight for Zac!

CHAPTER... ...FIVE

The rhino was getting closer and closer!

Then Zac thought about his Exo-skeleton suit.

It had a shield to protect him against anything.

Excellent, thought Zac. *I'm safe with this suit on.*

The rhino looked angry. It ran at Zac. Its horns were big and scary. Zac had the suit on but he stepped out of the way just in case!

The rhino hit the wall behind Zac.

Zac felt a tingle along his arms and legs. A recorded message on his suit said:

Muscle Power on

Zac walked up behind the rhino. He picked it up easily. It felt like picking up a feather.

This is a cool suit, thought Zac.

Zac put the rhino back in its cage. He locked the cage and looked around.

He saw Caz Rewop
running away. Caz
worked for BIG, the
evil spy group.

'Hello, Agent Rock
Star,' yelled Caz. 'I've
opened the zoo gates!

And I've let the lions out of their cage,' Caz laughed. She was evil.

Zac chased after Caz. He was fast in the suit.

Zac zoomed along the path. He nearly caught Caz. Then he heard a huge **ROAR!**

Two lions were heading for the zoo gates!

Zac looked at the lions. Then he looked at Caz. She was still laughing at him. Zac knew he had to get the lions.

Zac ran towards the lions. He jumped over

them and quickly
closed the gates. Then
he turned around to
face the lions. They
roared at him.

ROAR!

Zac grabbed the lions.
He held them up. Zac's
suit still said 'Muscle

Power On.' He was
so strong.

'I love this suit!' he
said to the lions.
'You're so light, you
feel like two little
kittens!'

Zac zoomed over to the
cage and dropped
the lions in. Then he
locked it shut.

Now Zac needed to
get Caz. He ran and
then jumped right
over the seal pool.
He landed in a big
open area.

But where was Caz?

Zac heard a loud noise
and looked up. He saw
a chopper about to
land. It had BIG in
big letters on it. Then
he saw Caz. She was
running to the chopper.

Oh no, Zac thought. *It's too late. She's getting away!*

Zac sped up. He was running faster than a speeding car!

The chopper landed and Caz started to get in.

'You'll never catch me, Agent Rock Star!' Caz yelled above the noise.

'Not even with that new suit of yours!'

Zac kept running. The chopper was off the ground now. Zac took a HUGE jump. He could almost reach the chopper.

Caz screamed to the pilot, **_GO HIGHER! HURRY!_**

Zac's fingers touched the chopper. Then he fell to the ground.
He had just missed her.

Zac watched Caz fly away. *Well, no-one got hurt*, Zac thought.
I'll catch her one day!

CHAPTER... ...SIX

Zac sat on the grass
and got out his iPod.
He put his headphones
on. Zac turned on
his favourite song.

He turned it up
as loud as it could go.
Then Zac checked his
pockets. He found a
Choc-Mallow Puff.
It was just what he
needed after all
that running.

Suddenly, Zac's
song stopped playing.

Zac looked at his iPod.
It was still working.
Then he heard a voice
in his headphones.
It was Leon.

'Great work, Zac,'
said Leon. 'But where's
my test drive report?'

Zac pulled out his
SpyPad.

He began to fill out his report.

Zac's iPod began playing his song again.

How does Leon do it? Zac thought. *He knows everything. And he seems to be everywhere!*

Zac pushed **send** on his SpyPad. Test drive

report done! Zac zoomed back to the school oval. He had to get back to the GIB Test Labs.

I'm going to miss this Exo-skeleton suit, he thought. *But not those stinky armpit bombs!*

TEST DRIVE
REPORT
PIT STINK BOMBS
Rating:
⬤⬤⬤⬤⬤

Smell:
⬤⬤⬤⬤⬤

The smell was so bad! I thought I was
going to pass out.

EXO-SKELETON SUIT
Rating:
⬤⬤⬤⬤⬤

Power:
⬤⬤⬤⬤⬤

This suit was awesome.
It helped me so much. Can I keep it?
END

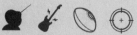

...THE END...